3800 18 0035629 1

HIGH

SADDLE

D1368931

The Grey Pony

Written by Lisa Thompson

Illustrated by Molly Sage

Blake

EDUCATION

Better ways to learn

Saddleback Stables: The Grey Pony
ISBN: 978 1 76020 168 5

 Lexile®Measure: 690L
For more information visit www.lexile.com
Lexile © 2013 MetaMetrics, Inc.

Text copyright © 2018 Lisa Thompson
Written by Lisa Thompson
Illustrations copyright © 2018 Blake Publishing
Illustrated by Molly Sage

Published by Blake Education Pty Ltd
ABN 50 074 266 023
108 Main Road
Clayton South VIC 3169
info@blake.com.au
www.blake.com.au

Publisher: Katy Pike
Series editor: Mark Stafford
Page layout: Modern Art Production Group
Printer: 1010 Printing Asia Limited

This publication is © copyright. No part of this book may be reproduced by any
means without written permission from the Publisher.

CONTENTS

Chapter One
To Wombat Flat   5

Chapter Two
The Pit Ponies   10

Chapter Three
Here to Help   26

Chapter Four
Protected   40

Pony Profile   46

Glossary   48

Jordy

Chief

Sophie

Peaches

Hannah

Jin Jin

Bella

Gypsy Rose

Alexa

Billy Blaze

CHAPTER ONE

To Wombat Flat

Hannah was **giddy** with excitement. Her friend Bella had invited her on an all-day trail ride to Wombat Flat. After weeks of riding lessons at Saddleback Stables, Hannah couldn't wait for a ride in the bush.

Hannah arrived at the stables early with a packed lunch and water bottle. When she got to the tack room, she discovered her pony's riding gear was missing.

"Hey, hope you don't mind, Hannah. We got Jin Jin ready for you."

Hannah turned and saw her friend

Jordy at the tack room door. Behind him was Sophie.

Jordy and Sophie were in Hannah's Saturday riding class. Jordy was the best rider in the group and rode a pony called Chief. Sophie rode a palomino pony called Peaches. Chief, Peaches and Jin Jin were **School ponies** that belonged to Saddleback Stables. Yet Jordy, Sophie and Hannah spent so much time riding and caring for them that they felt like their own.

"We're all going on the trail ride?" **squealed** Hannah.

"Wouldn't miss it," said Jordy. "Grab a helmet and let's go. I put a saddle pack on Jin Jin, so you can put your lunch and water in there."

"I've never been to Wombat Flat," said Sophie. "Have you, Jordy?"

Jordy nodded. "It's an open area about the size of two football fields. It's great for riding. Wombat Flat looks down into Ghost Gum Gully and back along Saddleback Ridge. You can see the dip in the ridge that looks like a saddle."

Bella suddenly appeared at the doorway. "Great, you're all here. I've been racing around getting Gypsy Rose ready," she **panted**.

"You sure you don't want to take Reba?" asked Sophie. "Wouldn't she be better on the trail?"

Reba was the school pony Bella learned to ride on before she got Gypsy Rose, her strawberry roan pony.

"Charlie thinks Gypsy Rose will be fine," replied Bella. "We all ready?"

"Who's Charlie?" Hannah asked.

"She's my cousin," said Bella. "She's taking us on the trail. She used to work here as a stablehand."

"Charlie's an excellent rider," added Jordy.

"Charlie's over there, talking to Miss Jill." Bella pointed to her cousin and the owner of Saddleback Stables.

Hannah noticed a **striking**, dark-brown horse with **white socks** tied up near Miss Jill's house.

"That's Charlie's horse, Duke," said Jordy. "He looks strong and alert, doesn't he, like a racehorse."

Charlie waved Miss Jill goodbye and trotted over on Duke.

"Okay, you lot," she said, slowing as she went by, "let's do this."

Jin Jin whinnied and needed only the slightest tap from Hannah to get moving. Like everyone else he was keen for a day in the bush.

CHAPTER TWO

The Pit Ponies

Charlie halted at the beginning of the track and turned Duke to face her riders. She sat relaxed in the saddle, and Duke stood calmly. He knew he was a fine horse with a very good rider.

"Just a reminder not to go off the track," said Charlie. "There are all kinds of things, like wombat holes, rocks and tree roots, which can **lame** your pony or worse. The first section is a pretty easy ride, nice and wide, so we'll do some cantering. Then the trail gets steep, so slow it down. Some of you may want to **dismount**,

depending on how your pony handles it. The trail then narrows before we come out at Wombat Flat for a good gallop. Everybody ready?"

"You bet!" said Jordy. Chief **pawed** at the ground, **shifting** his weight from one hoof to the other.

Hannah gulped. Wombat holes? Tree roots? She'd never dismounted mid-trail or scrambled over rocks with Jin Jin. And she wasn't sure Jin Jin would want to gallop after a long, hard ride.

"Now, there's no rush, Jordy," Charlie said and smiled.

The group followed her and Duke single file into the bush. Chief snorted when Gypsy Rose and Bella tried to pass—he clearly wanted to be behind

Duke. Bella pulled Gypsy Rose into line. Hannah followed on Jin Jin, and Sophie wandered along last on Peaches.

The bush closed behind the riders. Morning light filtered through the trees and dappled the track. Hannah felt like they had entered another world, or stepped back in time. They could be bushrangers on the run, or drovers seeking lost cattle. She smiled knowing Jordy would love the idea of being a bushranger, charging through the bush on the back of the **bold** and **strong** Chief.

The group turned a bend and the track opened out to a grassy area with few trees. Charlie looked over her shoulder briefly.

"Let's pick up the pace," she nodded, and encouraged Duke into a canter.

The rest followed and the sound of hooves thundered across the clearing. Hannah couldn't wipe the smile off her face. The ground beneath her blurred and the cold morning air streamed past. There was nothing as exciting as riding in the wild.

After a while, they dropped the canter back to a trot and finally a walk to the far side of the clearing. Duke and the ponies were **puffed** but happy.

Hannah looked behind her. "Hey, where's Sophie and Peaches?"

All the riders turned to see where the **stragglers** had got to. Sophie appeared in a bouncy trot on her palomino pony and then pulled up to a walk.

"Peaches wasn't so keen on the canter," she said with a huff. The palomino nudged her way past Jin Jin and Gypsy Rose and stopped behind Chief.

"Walk on!" called Charlie and she and Duke continued back into the bush.

"Hey Charlie," said Bella, "I told

Grandpa you were taking us up to Wombat Flat and he said I had to keep an **eye out** for the grey pony that protects the track."

Charlie laughed. "There's no pony protecting the track, Bella. That's just one of Grandpa's stories."

"I know the story about the pony called Ghost," said Jordy. "We learnt about it at school as part of local history. Ghost worked in the coalmine at Ghost Gum Gully. He was a bit of a **hero** but that was ages ago."

"See!" protested Bella. "Grandpa didn't make it up."

"No, he didn't make that story up," said Charlie. "There was a pit pony called Ghost, like Jordy said, but that was a long, long time ago." She glanced over her shoulder at Bella and then back at the track. Charlie shook her head. "Any pony that Grandpa saw would have just been lost. If it was grey, that's just a coincidence. I don't think a grey pony hangs around protecting the track."

"Well, I believe him," said Bella, "and the pony that protects this path could be in the bush right now, watching us."

Charlie rolled her eyes. "Well, I hope it can keep up with me!" She squeezed her leg to tell Duke to canter. The others broke into a canter too, keen to keep up. The bush **whipped** past. Jin Jin panted and snorted from the effort. When they slowed down, Hannah noticed his coat was **streaked** with sweat.

The canter ended with the riders in two groups. Jordy was slightly ahead with Charlie, while the girls rode a little further back.

"It's a shame Charlie doesn't believe Grandpa's story," Bella said.

"What did she mean when she said 'pit pony'?" asked Hannah. "Is that something to do with their coat or **markings**?"

"No," replied Bella, "it's what they did. Years and years ago, there was a coalmine on the other side of Ghost Gum Gully. Grandpa worked there when he was young. Everyone around here did. The miners used ponies to carry the coal. They were called pit ponies."

"You mean ponies went underground?" asked Sophie.

"Yes," said Bella, "like the miners. They worked long hours underground in tight, dark spaces. One of the ponies was called Ghost. Grandpa said he got his name because of his grey body, white muzzle and mane, and light grey markings around his eyes. In the darkness of the mine he looked like a ghost. Grandpa said Ghost was a

gentle, hardworking pony but he could be a bit stubborn."

"Sounds like you, Jin Jin," said Hannah. "What happened to Ghost?"

"Ghost had a way of knowing when danger was about," Bella continued. "One day he **refused** to enter a tunnel, and the tunnel collapsed soon after. It was like he _knew_. The miners began to rely on Ghost to tell them if it was safe to work. In the evenings and on weekends, Ghost and the other pit ponies rested in the mine's paddocks. The miners really looked after them. Their lives depended on those ponies.

"But when new owners took over the mine, **everything changed**. They said the ponies had to stay underground, like they were just **pieces of equipment**. The ponies would only come out for some weekends. Grandpa and the other miners thought this was cruel and dangerous. The ponies worked hard and deserved their time above ground."

"How awful," said Sophie softly.

"The new mine owners built an underground stable," said Bella. "When it was time for the pit ponies to be moved there, Ghost **refused** to enter the mine. He disappeared into the bush with some of the other ponies and was never seen again. A few days later there was a big explosion right where the underground stable was. The mine collapsed. Grandpa said Ghost knew all along."

"What does this pit pony have to do with saving your Grandpa?" asked Hannah.

"Well, a couple of years ago Grandpa was riding up this same track to Wombat Flat, when a pony the same colour as Ghost suddenly appeared on the track. It scared the tail off Horrie, Grandpa's horse. Horrie shied and took off into the bush. Grandpa glanced back and saw a huge boulder on the track, right where he would have ridden. He would have run right into it! The grey pony had saved them both.

"But Horrie was so **spooked** that he then threw Grandpa and bolted. Grandpa was off the track and lost. It was getting late and he worried he wouldn't find the track before dark. Suddenly, the grey pony appeared again. It wouldn't let him get too close, but by following it Grandpa ended up at Cockatoo Creek. He then followed the creek back to town. Old Horrie turned up the next day.

"Grandpa reckons if it wasn't for that pony, he could have been wandering around in the bush for days. Getting lost in the bush is **no joke**."

"Wow!" said Hannah. "You think that pony was Ghost?"

"Grandpa said it sure looked like him, but Ghost would have been sixty years old by then. We all know ponies don't live that long, so it must have been …"

"Ghost's ghost!" said Sophie.

As the girls giggled, the thud of hooves grew closer and Charlie and Duke appeared.

"Come on, you lot!" called Charlie. "**Keep up**. This is a ride, not a stroll."

CHAPTER THREE

Here to Help

The riders began to climb a ridge. Cockatoos screeched and took off skyward, their cries echoing through the bush. Parts of the trail were muddy from earlier rain. The cool morning breeze carried the smell of dirt and wet leaves.

Through gaps in the bush Hannah could see an endless roll of treetops beneath her, either side of the track. The track was **flanked** by ferny undergrowth dotted with tall gum trees. Strips of brown and orange bark hung from the trees, revealing smooth, **silver-grey** trunks.

The riders walked, trotted and cantered at times. As the track narrowed and grew steeper, they slowed to walk in single file.

The noisy birds and muddy trail didn't bother Jin Jin. He was relaxed and happy, offering the occasional contented snort. But as the track dipped and two great trees arched over it, Jin Jin stopped. He pulled up so quickly that Gypsy Rose almost ran into him. The others ahead continued walking, but Jin Jin's ears **twitched** and he **sniffed** the morning air.

"What's wrong?" asked Bella.

"I don't know," said Hannah. "Walk on, Jin Jin." She gave him a little kick and clicked her tongue. Jin Jin stayed put.

"Move it, Jin Jin," said Bella. Gypsy Rose snorted.

Bella tried to get her pony to pass, but Gypsy Rose wouldn't move. Hannah and Bella were **stuck** on their stubborn ponies. The riders up ahead didn't notice and soon disappeared into the bush.

Hannah was about to call out to Charlie but her voice caught in her throat when a grey pony leapt onto the track in front of them. Jin Jin and Gypsy Rose both shied. They reared onto their hind legs, and both girls **tumbled off** their ponies into the steep, ferny gully beside the track.

They rolled down the gully, cushioned by the soft ferns and moss. Immediately there was a loud crack

29

and crashing noise, like a tree branch falling to the ground, followed by the sounds of Jin Jin and Gypsy Rose whinnying and thundering away.

Hannah opened her eyes. She lay on the ferns, listening to her heartbeat **thumping** in her ears. Her palms stung from the fall but apart from that she felt okay—nothing broken or sprained.

"What just happened?" she said, slowly sitting up.

"Hannah! HANNAH!"

Bella was calling. Hannah scanned the bush but couldn't see her.

"Bella!" yelled Hannah. "Where are you?"

"Over here. Behind you."

Hannah soon saw Bella's blue riding helmet and **dirt-stained** face coming toward her through the ferns. She was grinning.

"Did you see that pony, Hannah? Did you see? It was a grey pony, just like the one Grandpa saw! And just after it appeared, did you hear that branch come down? It would have fallen on our heads. The pony saved us!"

Hannah stood up slowly and looked around. "That branch sure sounded like a big one, and close too. Are you alright, Bella?"

Bella nodded. "I'll probably have a few bruises tomorrow but I'm fine."

"Good, same here. Where do you think Jin Jin and Gypsy Rose are?" Hannah **whistled** into the bush and called "Jin Jin!"

"Gypsy Rose!" called Bella. "Gypsy!"

Hannah looked around. There was no sign of Jin Jin or Gypsy Rose or the grey pony … or of the track. The fall had confused her. The bush all looked the same.

"Um, Bella, do you know which way the track is?"

"It's over there," said Bella, pointing to her left. "No, wait." She **jerked** her head in the opposite direction and pointed. "Maybe I rolled down from there."

"That grey pony might have saved us from the falling branch," said Hannah, "but now I think we're lost."

"Don't be silly. We're not lost," said Bella, looking into the trees. "We just don't know where we are … exactly."

"That's called lost," **mumbled** Hannah. She whistled for Jin Jin again. Nothing. "If Jin Jin and Gypsy Rose ran back the way we came, Charlie and the others won't know what happened to us."

"We can't be lost," said Bella. "I don't want to be lost. Charlie! CHARLIE!"

Bella's call sounded very loud in the bush. No call came back. The silent bush suddenly felt very, very big and empty.

"What should we do?" asked Bella, beginning to sound **panicky**.

"Shhh," said Hannah suddenly. "I think I hear something."

Hannah and Bella **froze**. There was the occasional bird twitter. A light breeze made the leaves whisper. And there was the low rumbling of breathing … Both girls knew that sound. It was a pony.

Hannah and Bella slowly turned around to see two twitching, grey-tipped ears behind the ferns. A grey pony with a white mane pushed aside

the branches and stepped forward.
She had gentle eyes. She nickered and
dipped her head as she walked towards
the girls and sniffed them.

Hannah and Bella slowly raised their
hands and patted the pony. The filly
nickered **contentedly**.

"You knew that branch was going to fall, didn't you?" whispered Bella. "You saved us. You saved us just like Ghost saved the miners and that other pony saved my Grandpa." The pony **Snorted**. "Hannah, maybe when Ghost ran off from the coalmine he started a family of his own. That would make this pony his granddaughter, just like I'm Grandpa's."

"Maybe," said Hannah.

Bella looked into the pony's black eyes. "Do you think you could show us the way back to the others?"

The pony jerked her head up and the girls stepped back to give her space. She turned in the undergrowth and walked slowly away. When both girls stayed put, she stopped and whinnied, as if to say, "Well, are you coming?"

"Let's go," said Bella, starting after the grey pony. "She's going to show us the way."

"Or get us even more lost," muttered Hannah.

The **Sure-footed** pony weaved her way around trees, rocks and tree roots.

"It feels like we're going down," said Hannah, breaking into a jog to keep up. "Shouldn't we be going up?"

"We can't lose her," said Bella. "I'm sure she knows the way."

They **weaved** along the gully and then **scrambled** up a bank. Finally the pony stopped at the bottom of a steep, overgrown track.

"This might lead us to the Wombat Flat track," said Bella.

"How can you be sure?" said Hannah. "We've walked so far. It could lead anywhere."

The little pony **nibbled** on some young plants. She flicked her nose and grunted.

"No, I trust her," said Bella. "This is the way. She wants us to start climbing."

The sound of hooves **vibrated** from above and a familiar voice rang out. "Bella! Hannah!"

"Charlie!" cried the girls together. "Charlie, it's us! Can you hear us?"

Bella and Hannah immediately began climbing the track, shouting Charlie's name.

"Wait!" said Hannah after a dozen steps. "I want to thank the pony. Bella, you were right—she did save us. Twice."

Hannah and Bella looked back down the track but the grey pony was gone.

CHAPTER FOUR

Protected

"What happened?" asked Charlie, her voice a mixture of worry and relief at finding Hannah and Bella. "Are you alright?"

The girls nodded as they picked sticks and prickles off their clothes. "We're fine," said Bella. "Just a few scratches."

"Jin Jin and Gypsy Rose came **flying** past without you," Charlie explained. "Jordy went after them, while Sophie and I rode back along the track. There was no sign of you, just a branch blocking the track."

Jordy and Chief appeared from around

the bend, leading Jin Jin and Gypsy Rose. The ponies were **puffed** and **sweaty**, as were Jordy and Chief from the chase.

"What happened?" asked Jordy as he dismounted. He unclipped the pony's lead ropes from Chief's saddle and handed them to Hannah and Bella.

"Jin Jin and Gypsy Rose were startled by that falling branch," Bella said as she climbed back onto Gypsy Rose. "Isn't that right, Hannah?"

Hannah nodded and mounted Jin Jin. "You must have heard the huge cracking sound when it fell."

"No, we didn't hear a thing," said Sophie. "It took us a while to realise you weren't following us."

"Bella and I fell down into the gully," continued Hannah. "Lucky it was all soft and ferny."

"This is a really hard track to just stumble upon," said Charlie. "You two were very lucky to find it."

"No, we had help," said Bella. Jordy and Sophie looked at each other. They knew there was more to this story.

Bella shrugged. "Sometimes things happen that you wouldn't believe, Charlie. We were saved by a pony the same colour as Ghost, just like the one who saved Grandpa."

"Twice," added Hannah. "The pony saved us from the falling branch and then showed us the way back to the track."

"Oh, honestly," sighed Charlie, not believing either of them. "I don't know how you found the track again, but let's just get to Wombat Flat. And can we stay together this time? I don't want anything else to happen."

"Sure," said Bella smiling, "but if something does happen I think we'll be fine. After all, this is a protected track."

Everyone **nudged** their ponies into a walk.

"Thank goodness you're safe, Jin Jin," said Hannah, running her fingers through his mane. Jin Jin bobbed his head and chomped his bit. "And thank you, grey pony," Hannah whispered. She had a feeling the ghost pony—and maybe its family—was nearby, keeping watch.

PONY PROFILE

Name: Ghost

Rider: none

Owner: none

Age: unknown

Breed: Shetland pit pony

Height: 10 hands high

Temperament: helpful, cautious, wise

Coat: dappled grey (flecked grey and white)

Markings: white muzzle, white mane, white tail, grey markings around eyes

Habits: hiding in the undergrowth, warning riders of danger

Likes: quiet, the bush, other pit ponies and helping people avoid danger

Dislikes: stables, paddocks, loud noises and open country

Did you know? The earliest record of a pit pony working in Britain was at Durham Mine in 1750. Strong and hardy, pit ponies carried heavy loads and pulled carts of coal. They were small, to suit the cramped conditions of a mine. Their excellent instinct, sense of smell and hearing helped them sense danger. There are many tales of ponies rescuing injured miners and warning of catastrophes. Ponies stabled underground lived only three or four years.

GLOSSARY

dappled
covered with lighter or darker spots

filly
a young female horse or pony

nicker
a soft, breathy whinny

shied
moved suddenly sideways or backwards in fright

sure-footed
unlikely to stumble or trip

tack
riding equipment, such as saddles and bridles